Harriet Ziefert

HOME
FOR
NAVIDAD

Paintings by Santiago Cohen

HOUGHTON MIFFLIN COMPANY BOSTON 2003

Walter Lorraine (wr) Books

To Lillian, my beloved niece, and all the children in Mexico
who wait for their mothers, or fathers, to return.
And to Ethel, Diego and Isabel, whom I love with all my heart.
—S.C.

Walter Lorraine *ur* Books

Text copyright © 2003 by Harriet Ziefert
Illustrations copyright © 2003 by Santiago Cohen

www.houghtonmifflinbooks.com

Library of Congress Cataloging-in-Publication Data
Ziefert, Harriet.
  Home for Navidad / Harriet Ziefert : illustrations by Santiago Cohen.
    p. cm.
  Summary: Ten-year-old Rosa hopes that her mother, whom she has not seen
for three years, will leave her job in New York and come home to Santa
Catarina, Mexico, for Christmas and maybe even longer. Includes a
glossary of Spanish words used.
    ISBN 0-618-34976-6
  [1. Mothers and daughters—Fiction. 2. Alien labor—Fiction. 3.
Christmas—Fiction. 4. Santa Catarina (San Luis Potosai,
Mexico)—Fiction. 5. Mexico—Fiction.] I. Cohen, Santiago, ill. II. Title.
  PZ7.Z487Ho 2003
  [E]—dc21
                                        2002156430

Printed in China for Harriet Ziefert Inc.
HZI 10 9 8 7 6 5 4 3 2 1

My name is Rosa and I am ten.

I just woke up in the dark.

My grandmother is
already in the yard.
Everyone else calls her
Doña Juanita, but to
me she is *Abuela*.

When I open my eyes, the sound of her *metate* grinding corn is what I hear.

Abuela is making *tamales* and *atole* for breakfast. I wish I could stay in my bed a little longer, but I hear her calling, "*Arriba, Rosita, que ya amaneció.* Get up, Rosa, the sun is rising."

After break-
fast, I walk up
the road with my
little brother, Juan.
The field boss is
handing out big burlap sacks.

"*Ándenle!*" he is yelling.
"Get a move on."
Usually, I go
to the market with
Abuela and other
women, but today
I wanted to pick
corn with Tío
Pancho, my uncle.

Abuela gave me permission to go to
the fields with him until it was time for
school.

I stay close to Tío Pancho, who once
crossed the border to work in an orange
grove in California. He came back with
money to help Abuela pay for our house.

The boss sends us to the biggest field. We're lucky that
there's an early-morning breeze. By eleven o'clock, when Juan
and I leave for school with the rest of the *niños*, the heat will be
terrible, but the men will work until it's almost dark.

"Stick with me," says Tío Pancho. "I'll get the ears that are
high up, and you get the ones that are down low."

Now that we're alone, I ask, "Is Mama coming soon?"

Uncle Pancho says, "So that's why you're here today. You wanted to ask me when your mama was coming back."

"Sí...she's been gone so long...three whole years. I haven't seen Mama since my seventh birthday. I need to see her."

Tío Pancho agrees, "It's been long." But he adds, "When I talked to her on the phone, she said she is working extra... cleaning houses...so she can come home for *Navidad*."

Tío Pancho and I work quietly. The sun is up and the fields are getting hotter and hotter. My hands are starting to hurt. Tío Pancho knows what to do to make me feel better.

"Let's sing," he says, "and before you know it, it will be time for school."

Ay, ay, ay, ay,
Canta y no llores,
Porque cantando se alegran,
Cielito lindo, los corazónes.

Ay, ay, ay, ay,
Sing and don't cry,
Because singing my darling,
Makes your heart glad.

When the pickup truck comes, all the niños line up.
The dirt roads are bumpy, but the ride to school is short.

I decide not to tell Juanito, my brother, what Tío Pancho said. I want to keep it a secret...a secret just for me, Rosa.

Señora Garcia's math lesson makes me think of Mama. She asks: "If a man saves two hundred *pesos* every week, how many weeks will it be until he can buy a plane ticket for three thousand pesos?"

I know Mama sends *dólares* to Abuela. I want her to stay in Santa Catarina after Navidad, but I worry that if she does, we won't have enough money. But I'd rather have Mama than money.

When I get home from school, I go to the river with Abuela to wash clothes. I don't like scrubbing, but I like to rinse the clothes until the soap's all out.

Sometimes I pretend to be busy, but I'm really trying to hear what my grandmother's friends are talking about.

I hear "*Nueva York*" and I lean over to listen. Grandma is saying, "It's expensive to live in New York City, where Blanca works, so she rents a room in the Bronx."

But not for long, I say to myself.

When we get home, a letter is lying on the floor.
I recognize the stamps from *los Estados Unidos*.

Querida Rosa,   Monday

I hurt my back moving furniture and had to go to the doctor. I was worried I couldn't get to Santa Catarina for Navidad, but the doctor says I'll be okay.

I saved enough money for a plane ticket...now I'm working hard to have little extra, then I'm going to buy the ticket...one-way to Mexico City!

I hope you remember me with the same love that I remember you.

Muchos besos,
Mama Blanca

P.S. It's only 10 weeks to Christmas. What should I bring you? Sneakers? Earrings? Magazines?

"**Mama's coming!**"
I shout. "Mama's really
coming for Navidad!
And she's going to stay
in Santa Catarina."

"Don't count your
chickens," says Abuela.
"It's still a long way off.
And right now, I need you
to help me prepare dinner.
You know Pancho doesn't
like to wait."

Tío Pancho comes home with more good news. The corn crop has been *muy grande,* and there will be extra work and extra pay for everyone.

"Does that mean when Mama comes home from New York, she won't have to go back?"

"That is our hope," says Tío Pancho. "But if we need extra money, I will go to California to work on a farm and your mama can stay here with you and Juan."

After dinner, I write Mama a letter.

Thursday

Dear Mama:

School is good. I am learning to solve word problems in math. I know enough English to pick out lots of words in the magazines you sent me. Yes, I want you to bring more magazines when you come back. And earrings, too, please.

You have been gone for three whole years and I am afraid you won't recognize me when you get here.

I will be good and I promise not to make any extra work or trouble for Abuela.

I miss you.

Muchos besos,
Rosa

Abuela reminds me that it's time for bed.

For once, I have a good dream.

It is Navidad, a day for miracles, and I am in the market. It is crowded with people and all kinds of dogs. There is lots of food...*enchiladas, quesadillas, tamales,* and lots of sweets—*flan, ponche,* and *dulces*...all to share for Navidad.

The sky is exploding with fireworks. But the dogs are not scared and neither am I. We are used to the noise of Navidad.

A woman comes toward me. She is taller and prettier than all the other *madres*. And she says, "Rosa, I am here to stay."

SPANISH WORDS USED

abuela—grandmother
ándenle—get moving
arriba—get up
atole—corn meal hot drink
besos—kisses
casa—house
dólares—American money
dulces—sweets
enchiladas—Mexican spicy food
    made with tortillas and hot sauce
escuela—school
flan—custard dessert
gracias—thank you
grande—big
los Estados Unidos—the United States
madre—mother
metate—grinding stone
muchos—a lot of
muy—very
Navidad—Christmas
niños—children
pesos—Mexican money
ponche—fruit cider
querida—my dear
quesadillas—folded tortillas with cheese
que ya amaneció—it's daybreak
señora—a married woman
sí—yes
tamales—corn meal cake
tío—uncle
tortilla—corn meal pancake